Lottie Dale grew up in South London, attending school in Wimbledon before training as a nurse at St Bartholomew's Hospital. She was a health visitor and health promotion specialist prior to moving into senior management.

Lottie took up skydiving in her 30's and was part of a UK Freefall Record jump in 1989 and a British Women's Formation Record in 1994.

Always fascinated by words and passionate about cats, she has brought the two together in this, her first, publication.

Lottie's partner, artist Paul Priestley, has provided the book's illustrations.

She has three sons and two granddaughters.

Rory – The Purl Cat is dedicated to my beautiful granddaughters, Sophie and Luna, and my wonderful honorary grandchildren, Dulcie, Aurelia and Digby.

Lottie Dale

RORY – THE PURL CAT

Illustrated by: Paul Priestley

AUSTIN MACAULEY PUBLISHERS™

LONDON • CAMBRIDGE • NEW YORK • SHARJAH

A CIP catalogue record for this title is available from the British Library.

ISBN 9781398451674 (Paperback)
ISBN 9781398451681 (ePub e-book)

www.austinmacauley.com

First Published 2022
Austin Macauley Publishers Ltd®
1 Canada Square
Canary Wharf
London
E14 5AA

Chapter 1
Best Friends

He didn't mean to go when he did. In fact, the decision was taken completely out of his paws. There was so much more to do, to see, to experience.

The family called him Rory. He knew he was extremely good-looking – they would say, "what a beautiful boy" and compliment his fine tail and gorgeous, owl-like eyes.

Nothing much fazed Rory except small people with big voices. That would send him scurrying to hide until the shrill sounds stopped and normality was peacefully restored.

He would miss the family – but not as much, he suspected, as the family would miss him. Stupid lorry!

Still, it was time to move on. He made his way towards the glowing light – he knew he was looking for the Purl Flap.

And there it was right in front of him. Then he realised there was not one but two Flaps. One had a sign on it which read Tempurrary and the other said Purrmanent. He tried both Flaps but found the Purrmanent one wouldn't open so he turned to Tempurrary and pushed through.

He emerged at the bottom of a small Willow tree – with dangly branches touching the ground around him. Through the softly moving leaves, he saw a green garden with bushes and brightly coloured flowers. Goodness, what bliss! Suddenly, his ears were assailed by a sustained and very high-pitched screeching sound. His eyes closed and his muscles tensed as he prepared to swiftly exit the situation. But where to go? Everything was so unfamiliar.

He heard a soothing voice.

"It's alright Ollie. I'm here. Just relax sweetheart – it's going to be okay."

The voice repeated itself several times and he felt reassured.

Opening his eyes, he saw the source of the squealing. A little boy with ginger hair, pale skin and wide green eyes was lying on the grass. Small person with a big voice! Not only that, there were also two feet encased in brown boots ferociously kicking up and down.

His first instinct was to run – and exit the garden without touching the grass! But somehow, with the sound of the calm voice echoing in his head, he felt there was something more important to do.

"It's okay Ollie, calm down, Mummy's here."

What a lovely sound.

He moved closer to the flailing feet and up towards the ginger hair. The wailing sound started to fade. He felt a hand on his head followed by a giggle, a sniff and a chuckle. The little hand tweaked his ear – it was almost pleasant.

"Oh look Ollie – a cat has come to see you! Isn't that lovely – I wonder where he came from?"

The small boy stopped the big noise and was tickling him under the chin in just that right place. He purred.

The boy rested his head on Rory's chest listening intently to the purring.

A man appeared and Ollie said, "Look, Daddy!"

The man replied, "Poor chap – he looks in a bit of a state. What do you think happened to him?"

Rory, although he was finding it hard to breathe with a heavy head resting on his chest, thought the owner of the ginger hair certainly didn't look in much of a state at all. In fact, with the shrill noise abated, he was quite handsome – just like himself.

"Hey, Ollie – why don't we go into the house it's nearly teatime?"

"Don't want to!" said small person firmly – raising his head momentarily. "Want to listen to cat."

Rory took this opportunity to spring to his feet – the thought of food now uppermost in his head.

Instantly, Ollie resumed his wailing whilst shouting, "Want cat, want cat."

Rory moved towards the distressed small person – and the kicking and flailing slowed – he felt the little hand on his ear followed by a head on his chest. He purred.

After a while, they all made their way slowly to the house. In the kitchen, Mum prepared sausages – which went down well with both!

After they had finished, Mum asked Ollie to lead the way upstairs to the bathroom – not a popular place with either small boy or cat.

More howls reached Rory's ears – but instead of sending him running, the sounds drew him in and he found himself sitting on the side of the bath whilst Ollie smiled and splashed.

Rory listened as Ollie's parents talked gently.

They said it was lovely that Ollie became calm around, "this poor chap", and that, "if he's staying, we ought to give him a name."

The name they chose was Kevin and Rory decided he was okay with that.

Kevin followed Ollie into his bedroom and sat purring as pyjamas were put on and hair reluctantly combed. His ear was tweaked several times.

Kevin noticed a large mirror on the wardrobe door. He liked mirrors; it was where he would admire his elegant reflection. He stepped forwards and turned to show off his best profile.

Oh! My Goodness! It wasn't a mirror but a window. He could see another cat. A creature with a bent and twisted ear, swollen eye, half a tail and several bald patches.

What should he do? Fight – but, being a bit of a coward, he really didn't like claw-offs? Or feel sorry that any cat could end up looking like this – and attempt to befriend it?

Kevin moved sideways – so did the creature. He moved the other way – so did the creature. He arched his back, brought his feet together, fluffed out his tail and hissed – so did the creature. He sat down – so did the creature.

It took a long time to get used to this new look. Eventually, his fur grew back, except around the tatty ear and his eye became less swollen, although it always leaked a tear or two even when he wasn't sad.

Visitors came to the house and looked at him with sad faces – their mouths taking on an 'O' shape. They didn't touch or tickle him under the chin – and certainly not behind his ragged ear.

Most people ignored him.

Ollie, however, loved stroking him, tweaking his good ear and listening to his purring. As time went by, the boy's head became heavier, so Kevin took to lying across his legs. Ollie felt the purring vibration with his hand – it would make him smile.

Ollie was uncomfortable with certain situations – unexpected noises and changes to his usual routine. He could become frustrated and overwhelmed even with mealtimes and bedtime – leading to a meltdown. Mum was always on hand to help with reassurance and a calming voice.

Kevin found he was often aware of an unsettling situation before Ollie became upset. He would nudge the lad with his head or paw and purr loudly. The two of them were inseparable. Each needing the other.

Mum bought a small harness and lead and Ollie would take his feline friend for walks around the garden. Kevin didn't mind the harness or being led by his special companion.

The two even travelled in the car, both safely strapped in the back.

A day dawned when Mum and Dad both looked extremely happy – smiling at Ollie – they even gave Kevin a stroke. The boy dressed himself in grey trousers and white shirt. Whilst holding Kevin's ear, his hair was combed and they both sat in the back of the car for a short journey. Ollie got out and Kevin returned home. Later that day, he again sat in the back of the car as Ollie was picked up and brought home.

This happened for many days. Kevin now had more time to himself. He wandered around the garden and would often snooze under the dangling branches of the now much bigger Willow tree.

Remembering the days with his old family, he wondered how they all were and if they still remembered him. Sometimes he glanced in the mirror at his rather bedraggled reflection and recalled the time when he was called, 'A beautiful boy'.

Somehow, it didn't seem to matter anymore – he felt content, needed and loved.

Many more days, weeks and months passed by. Ollie was missing from the house more often than he was there but he still spent a lot of time with Kevin.

The now elderly cat loved to see the lad's smile and sit across his lap feeling a considerably larger hand resting on his chest, tweaking his ear.

One day, Kevin opened his eyes from a deep sleep and gazed into the face of his best friend and companion. He was sure he could see a few ginger hairs starting to sprout from the handsome chin.

Ollie smiled and gently lifted Kevin into his arms. Two best friends sharing a special moment.

Not long afterwards, Kevin took a long nap under his favourite Willow tree. When he awoke it was early evening and the sun was setting. As his eyes became used to the growing darkness, he saw that he was once more in front of the two Purl Flaps.

He placed his paw on the one labelled Purrmanent, but again it was stuck or locked. So, he turned to the Tempurrary Purl Flap and pushed through.

Chapter 2
1666

Rory emerged from the Purl Flap with a feeling of excitement. He felt like a new cat, all injuries repaired and full of energy. It was dark and a strong, warm wind nearly blew him off his feet.

Although night, his sharp eyesight picked out a narrow lane where the rooftops on each side almost met in the middle. No one was around.

Rory noticed a glow in one of the windows and, as he watched, it became bigger and brighter.

Suddenly, one of the upstairs windows flung open and, with a lot of shouting, two men and a woman climbed out and started to make their way along the apex of the roof.

Rory was amazed. He was experienced at roof climbing but had never seen people attempting it and they weren't managing very well.

After several minutes of scrabbling, shouting, slipping and sliding, he was relieved to see the three climb back in through another window and, shortly afterwards, emerge onto the lane.

The glow in the house was clearly a fire and it was becoming bigger by the minute. The three continued yelling and people started to come out of the neighbouring houses. A few carried buckets of water to throw on the fire but there wasn't enough to deal with the growing blaze. Flames were now shooting through the roof, jumping the short gap and setting fire to houses on the other side of the lane.

More people came out, loading their belongings onto wooden carts and moving away from the growing heat and smoke.

Rory thought it would be helpful if he led the panicking people away from the increasing danger. The smoke and heat were alarming and soon he found he had outrun everyone and was once more on his own.

The wind remained strong and within a few minutes the smoke and heat had caught up with him. He jumped as the bells in a large church tower started to clang. Even more people rushed out to see what was happening.

As he waited, the people pushing carts arrived, trying to catch their breath, before heading off again.

Although still night, it was as bright as day and the crackle and roar of the flames were becoming louder.

Morning came and still the fire grew.

Rory saw old people being carried through the streets in their beds. One stopped close to him. The two pushing it were panting and the lady in the bed looked frightened. Rory saw that there were two small children in the bed tucked under the arms of its occupant.

Men, women and children were running around not knowing what to do.

A man rode up on a black horse. He shouted at a group of soot-covered men who began to break up nearby houses not yet damaged by the fire. Rory thought this was an odd thing to do. He heard the man on horseback, who was being called The Duke, say that, if the houses were knocked down, perhaps the fire couldn't burn them. It didn't work and the fire carried on its progress of destruction.

The smoke was making it hard to breathe and Rory's eyes were watering. In the distance he saw a wide river and ran towards it where the air seemed clearer. He saw crowds of people with black-smudged faces coughing, spluttering and wiping their eyes. Many were taking their belongings from the carts and throwing them into boats on the river. Most managed to miss the boats and their possessions ended up floating away or sinking into the water.

Without their precious things, people were able to escape more quickly. However, there was no bridge here to cross the river to safety, so the mass continued staying ahead of the advancing flames.

Rory found himself walking beside a lady he had seen throwing her whole cart into the river. She was clasping tightly to her chest the once white apron tied around her waist. Rory saw in the apron a clutch of fluffy baby chicks, her only remaining possession. The sight of these little creatures made Rory realise that he was hungry!

The lady's cherished chicks were not an option so an alternative solution was required. There was only one possible option. Rory had passed several pigeons who, having flown too close to the flames, had crashed to the ground amid singed feathers. He found one nearby. It tasted ghastly but took the edge off his hunger.

Feeling stronger, he trotted on at a lively pace. He did try jumping onto one of the beds being transported through the smoky streets but was swiftly shushed away.

Night returned and the chaos continued. Rory turned a corner and saw a group of young boys wearing school uniform and carrying leather buckets filled with water. A man was urging them onwards towards a church where a small fire had broken out. Rory watched as the boys emptied and refilled their buckets. They worked hard until the church was saved from the fire. The new day dawned still windy, smoky and smelly.

An impressive looking man appeared riding a large horse. Amid the confusion, people bowed their heads muttering, 'Your Majesty.'

King Charles urged the stampeding people to stop and fight the fire as it approached. He threw coins onto the ground as an incentive; one of which hit Rory and made him hiss. The King dismounted grabbing an implement which squirted water in an effort to help control the fire. Rory, normally inclined to stay clear of large animals, found himself perched on a wall next to the King's horse. They looked at each other and, in the dark brown eyes of the magnificent beast, Rory saw a mixture of fear and courage. The moment between them was brief before the King leapt back into the saddle and sped away.

Rory followed in the same direction. He saw a huge church in flames. The roof was melting, sending blobs of molten metal onto the ground. Suddenly, a ball of fire crashed over Rory's head making him flatten onto the ground. It shot across the road, through a window and exploded in a bright flash starting yet another fire.

Time to move on again.

Once more, hunger forced him to munch on roast pigeon. Just as he attempted to swallow one last mouthful of flesh and feathers, there came the loudest noise he had ever heard. Rory remembered the courage he had witnessed in the eyes of the King's horse. Although terrified, he moved forward to investigate the cause of the deafening sound.

He watched men working around a house not yet touched by the fire. They weren't knocking this one down and Rory found himself filled with curiosity. The workers moved away from the house, ducking down behind a nearby wall. With a huge flash of light and a massive sound, Rory saw the whole house leave the ground in an upward direction before crashing back down in a myriad of small pieces. His eyes and ears rang and rattled and even his teeth seemed to ache.

Rory left the scene. He heard further explosions as more houses were demolished in the path of the blaze. This time, the destruction of the buildings did provide a barrier to the progress of the fire. The end was in sight.

Another day dawned and the wind finally dropped allowing the flames to die down.

Rory tried to retrace his steps but the ground was so hot it burned his paws.

As he passed a building, he heard a pitiful sound. Hopping over the hot ash, Rory saw something emerge from the rubble of a chimney. It was another cat. His fur was scorched, one eye swollen and he walked with some difficulty.

He said his name was Sampey.

They made their way slowly to open ground where people were erecting tents. Creeping under the edge of one, they found an old blanket and soon the two were curled up together, sound asleep.

Well into the next day, hunger woke them. Rory was dreading another meal of pigeon, but he didn't need to worry. There was a plentiful supply of food for the people in the camp – and a good larder of leftovers for them. Sampey still had trouble walking so Rory brought a selection for him to sample.

Several days passed and Rory found himself recovering well. However, Sampey was not improving. He looked really uncomfortable and was now not eating the food offered to him.

Rory realised the time had come for Sampey to go to the Purl Flap. That night, as they curled up on their blanket, Rory looked beyond the edge of the tent and there they were – the two Purl Flaps. With a gentle nudge, he encouraged Sampey to stand and together they moved forward. Rory tried the Purrmanent Flap but it was still stuck shut. So he returned to the Tempurrary Flap and, side by side, they pushed through.

Chapter 3
A Toy Story

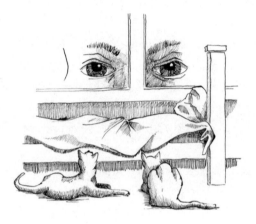

They tumbled through the Purl Flap at some speed.

Rory could see they had entered a living room. In one corner was an impressive and very colourful Barbie Dolls' House next to which was a matching Campervan.

As both cats completed their third roly poly, Rory became aware that the Dolls' House appeared to be getting larger – and they were heading directly for it. With a crash, they slid through the purple front door and screeched to a halt.

"What happened?" gasped Rory trying to catch his breath.

They peered out through the Dolls' House window and were amazed to see the rest of the living room was now huge.

"We've shrunk!" exclaimed Sampey.

Rory nodded with wide eyes. Sampey looked like a new cat. His fur had changed colour and his eyes shone emerald green.

"You're a ginger," Rory said and Sampey tilted his head to one side and winked.

Sampey stood, tail straight up in the air and said, "Well, look at you, Bro, totally tabby, don't you look the part!"

The boys grinned at each other and did a paw pump. It was then Rory noticed his front paws looked different. The pads were like small hands with neat little fingers instead of claws. Rory reached forward and picked up a ball from the floor. He tossed it to Sampey who caught it in his hand-like paw.

"Epic," yelled Sampey. "To me."

The two made their way into the living room.

"I fancy a kip," said Rory as he popped up onto a squashy sofa. "Snooze away Bro – I'm off to case the joint."

Rory rested his head on his pands, still fascinated by the ability to wiggle his fingers and do thumbs up. Soon he drifted into sleep.

Awoken by strange voices, he was about to shout to Sampey when he realised it was now dark. He saw a young lady and a large dog coming into the room.

The young lady reached forward, switching on a little table lamp, before jumping backwards and letting out a shriek of surprise. For a split second, time stood still before Rory made a dash for the door.

A throaty growl travelled from the big dog's chest to his mouth and emerged into the room. The force of which accelerated the cat's exit into the hall and up the white stairs.

"Sampey! Where are you?" wheezed Rory.

"Hey Dude, what's occurring?" slurred Sampey, waking from his slumber.

"We've been discovered and we need to get out of here QUICK! There's a large, growling dog after us!" hissed Rory, trying to keep both the volume and panic out of his voice.

"Follow me!" Sampey shot through an open door onto the balcony.

Rory accelerated behind him and didn't see Sampey screech to a halt. Unable to stop, Rory slammed into Sampey and both slid off the balcony onto a lilac slide spiralling downwards.

"Phew! Thank goodness that was there to break our fall," shouted Sampey.

Then SPLASH! They landed like two skimming stones across a pink swimming pool.

"I don't like water!" gurgled Rory, as he disappeared under the surface.

The two soggy moggies looked up at the balcony where the young lady and large dog were laughing at the scene below.

"We need to hide. Quick, over there!"

The cats raced around the side of the House towards the adjacent Campervan and jumped inside the open door.

Peering out of the window, they could see into the Barbie House where the young lady was loudly recounting the events to another.

"Then, Sophie, they slithered down the slide into our swimming pool – it was hilarious!"

"Oh stop, Dulcie, you're killing me!" replied Sophie.

The two were trying to apply makeup but without success as their hands were shaking with mirth.

Eventually, Sophie said, "Let's find Aurelia and Luna so that we can have some more fun before it gets light."

The bedraggled pair dried their fur on fluffy, pink towels – pands coming in useful again and curling up on the squashy bed, they fell asleep.

When they awoke, it was daytime. There was no sign of Dulcie and Sophie, but a pale brown horse and a colourful unicorn stood motionless outside the House.

Rory went to open the Campervan door when an enormous, little girl appeared and picked up the horse and unicorn. She made the horse gallop and jump over makeshift fences and then combed and plaited the long rainbow mane and tail of the unicorn.

Leaving the unicorn lying on its side, the enormous, little girl started to look around.

"Where are you?" she said approaching the Campervan.

"Yikes!" exclaimed Rory as he and Sampey dived under the bed.

Two huge eyes peered through the side window.

"Not there," she muttered.

Breathing a sigh of relief, the two emerged. They saw the enormous, little girl reach inside the house and pull-out Dulcie and Sophie one in each hand. The girls were also motionless although Rory thought that he saw a chink of recognition in Dulcie's eyes when her gaze rested briefly on the cats inside the Campervan.

The enormous, little girl played with Dulcie and Sophie for a while, changing their clothes into leotards and leg warmers.

Finally tiring of the games, the enormous, little girl went away leaving Sophie and Dulcie doing the splits, the horse sitting down like a dog and the unicorn still on its side. There was no sign of Digby the dog.

Rory and Sampey crept out to assess the situation. Nothing moved as they roamed around the house. Digby, they discovered, was balanced on his nose by his food bowl in the kitchen.

"This is strange," said Rory. "Why aren't they moving?"

"Search me Bro, perhaps they only move when it's dark." ventured Sampey.

"Yes, that's it," exclaimed Rory, "you're absolutely right. That's how the enormous, little girl can play with them."

"Whatever," replied Sampey, "but how about we get our own back on these guys for getting us wet yesterday?"

The two cats sniggered and enjoyed another pand pump.

Much later, as the light receded the pair watched as Dulcie and Sophie awoke from their daytime state.

The girls looked down at the clothes they had been given by the enormous, little girl.

"Oh, for goodness's sake," exclaimed Dulcie, "as if this body needs to go to the gym!"

Meanwhile, the horse and unicorn gathered themselves back onto their feet.

Rory, watching from the Campervan, noticed that the girls and animals had jointed limbs which enabled them to move around into different positions. The dog, pony and unicorn also had jointed tails. A plan was emerging.

Dulcie decided to ride Luna and Sophie attached Aurelia to a Princess Carriage to take her for a trot.

After a while, Aurelia announced that, as a unicorn, she should be able to fly. Increasing her speed to a gallop, the carriage suddenly left the ground and turned over. Sophie shot out and landed heavily close to the Campervan.

Sampey winced, "Ouch, poor thing!"

Before Rory could stop him, he rushed out to help. Luckily unharmed, Sophie thanked Sampey and started to stroke him.

"What a handsome cat," she purred.

Sampey also purred and curled himself around her legs.

"Psst psst," hissed Rory, "get back, it's not safe."

Reluctantly, Sampey obliged, but a bond had been formed.

As another day began, everyone except Rory and Sampey ceased moving.

The cats emerged from the Campervan and Rory explained his plan to achieve their revenge.

"I'm not sure Bro," said Sampey but Rory was determined, "we're really going to need our pands for this," he chuckled.

To support his friend, a reluctant Sampey agreed.

Having completed their preparations, the two returned to the Campervan for a cat-nap before nightfall.

However, their slumber was disturbed when the enormous, little girl reappeared. They watched the look of astonishment on her face as she saw all her toys with different limbs belonging to someone else.

Dulcie had little dog legs belonging to Digby. Sophie had two long legs belonging to Luna. Digby had his own front legs plus two long rear ones belonging to Aurelia. Aurelia also had her own front legs plus Dulcie's girlie legs at the rear. Luna had Sophie's legs and two of her own. Digby now has a long rainbow tail and Aurelia sported a doggie tail.

Peeking from their hiding place, Rory began to feel slightly guilty as he watched the enormous, little girl carefully reassemble her toys.

Beside him, Sampey smiled and gently nudged his friend.

"It was good Bro, time to move on."

Rory realised that something had changed.

Darkness fell and the enormous, little girl left to go to bed. Sampey opened the door of the Campervan and walked towards the awakening girls and animals.

As he sat beside Sophie, Rory saw that his friend now also had jointed legs and tail. Sophie put her hand on her new companion who purred loudly.

"It was truly great, Sampey – thank you for the adventure," said Rory.

Turning away from the open door, he saw a glow ahead of him and realised that he was back at the Purl Flaps.

He tried the Purrmanent Flap but it remained locked. So, without a backward glance, he returned to the Tempurrary Flap and pushed through.

Chapter 4
Mulovelly

Rory exited the Purl Flap straight into a rainstorm. Soaking wet, he searched for a place to shelter. Pretty little houses lined the steep road and he slithered down the slippery slope until he found a covered wood store in a flower-filled front garden.

Shaking the largest drops of water from his fur, Rory noticed that he now had a rich brown coat with mottled spotty effect.

"I look like a leopard," he mused to himself.

As he peered out of the wood store, two ungainly, young seagulls landed on the garden fence.

"What d'ya wanna do, Plodney?" said one.

"I dunno, what do YOU wanna do, Ronker?" replied Plodney.

"Let's chase cats," decided Ronker.

"Okay, but remember what happened last time?" muttered Plodney.

"It's stopped raining, the cats should be out shortly," declared Ronker.

Rory edged further back into the wood store trying to remain out of sight. A hissing sound assailed his ears and looking over his shoulder he beheld six pairs of eyes peering at him.

"Oh, I'm in your space, sorry – I'm just going," said Rory, dreading having to run out in front of the seagulls.

"Don't go – it's not a problem – are you new around here?" came the reply from a black cat with large golden eyes.

"Yes, I've just arrived – in fact I don't know where I am," returned Rory.

"You're in Mulovelly – it's a village by the sea. My name is Phoenix," said the black cat, "and this is Polly, Evie, Barney, Thomas and, lastly, Lady Arwen."

"I'm Rory and I'm really pleased to meet you, particularly as I've just heard those two large, young seagulls sitting on the fence." said Rory quietly.

"Ah, you've met Plodney and Ronker – not the brightest new kids in the flock," replied Phoenix.

"True," whispered Rory, "but they're planning to chase us and they're quite big."

"Ah yes, I remember what happened last time," mused Phoenix, "let the chase begin!"

Oh my goodness, thought Rory, as all the cats except Lady Arwen pushed passed him and raced onto the steep slope. The cats slid across the wet street attracting the attention of Plodney and Ronker who were busy practicing their seagull calls.

There followed a flash of feathers and fur, squawking and yowling. Up the hill and down again, the battle continued.

Rory remained motionless, not sure how to help his new friends. After several minutes, the squawling stopped and Rory crept forward to see what was left. Lady Arwen strolled passed him, tail straight up in the air. In front of them were all the cats. The posse had surrounded the two hapless seagulls who were cowering in the corner of the yard.

"That happened last time," said Lady Arwen.

Soon, bored with guard duty, the cats started to back off allowing Plodney and Ronker to regain some composure. They began to stretch their necks and flex their ruffled feathers. Rory was just thinking that the gulls were now looking a little overconfident, when a large brown and black dog appeared.

"Ooops, perhaps we're in trouble now!" Rory said to himself.

"Hi Kye," said Phoenix, "want to see these upstarts off?"

"My pleasure," returned the dog as he accelerated towards the two, barking loudly.

Plodney and Ronker had just enough room to execute an untidy take-off. Once safely on the roof, they began squawking at the top of their voices.

"We'll get you next time!"

"Doubt it!" responded Phoenix.

"Phew," said Rory, "how come Kye chased the gulls and not the cats?"

"Oh Kye's a good mate – we all get on really well in Mulovelly – except for the seagulls who steal our fish dinners," said Phoenix. "In fact, it was Kye who showed me the entrance to the Time Cave."

"Shhh," said the cat called Polly, "you're not supposed to talk about it!"

"Oh yes, I forgot – sorry," and that conversation ended there.

After the chase, life in the village carried on as usual. Rory found himself welcomed at the Mulovelly Cove Inn which sat next to a little harbour where the fishermen landed their catch – there was a plentiful supply of pilchards, crabs and lobster for the village felines.

Every week, the fishermen gathered in the Inn to sing sea shanties – Rory would hide under a table listening to tales of smugglers, storms and shipwrecks.

Several years passed by. Every spring, there would be the usual 'chase' with the new young seagulls – always with the same outcome.

One thing troubled Rory. His good friends Phoenix and Polly were often missing for weeks at a time. When they returned, they refused to say where they'd been.

"What's that all about," thought Rory.

Lady Arwen also spent a lot of time in the Inn – mostly sleeping as she was now quite old. She enjoyed telling Rory about the village.

However, Rory could not get her to talk about the disappearing Phoenix and Polly. All she would say was Phoenix was a bit of a rogue and Polly had an extra digit giving her big paws.

One evening, Lady Arwen regaled Rory with stories about cats and pirate ships. Apparently, a black cat was considered lucky on a pirate ship as they could protect the vessel from dangerous weather. They could, however, start a storm through magic contained in their tails. If a cat walked right up to a pirate, there would be good luck – but, if the cat turned around halfway, there would be bad luck. If a cat fell, or was thrown into the water, the ship would be cursed with misfortune and a massive storm.

Lady Arwen also mentioned that cats with extra digits on their paws were thought to be better at climbing on a pirate ship and very useful in catching rats and mice. Thinking about Polly, this last comment set Rory's mind racing but how could he encourage Lady Arwen to tell him more – he was sure she was not telling him everything.

Rory decided to share his secret with Lady Arwen.

One evening, as they both sat on the wall outside the Inn, Rory said, "Do you remember when I first arrived in Mulovelly?"

"It was just before that soggy chase with Plodney and Ronker, wasn't it?"

"Yes, that's right, but do you know how I got here?" asked Rory.

"You came through The Purl Flap," responded Lady Arwen.

"How did you know that!" exclaimed a startled Rory.

"Simple really, I'm a Purl Cat too," came the unexpected reply.

When Rory had recovered from this news, Lady Arwen explained that she had passed through the Purl Flap eight times. She recounted her adventures including being ship's cat on the Titanic where she had been called Jenny and then a railway cat called Skimbleshanks where she had been a boy.

"To be honest," she said, "I was relieved to arrive here where life is quiet and I've been able to stay for a long while."

Still shocked, Rory didn't feel able to ask Lady Arwen about Phoenix and Polly. So, village life resumed for a few more months. As autumn set in, the cats gathered around the empty lobsterpots in the harbour. The felines found this time of year a bit boring until the excitement of Christmas returned.

"What ya' wanna do?" said one young cat.

"Dunno, what YOU wanna do?" replied another youngster.

"Don't start, you two!" said Polly waving her big paw in the air.

Phoenix looked at Polly and mouthed, "Ready?"

The two cats moved off. Rory watched as Lady Arwen appeared from behind the lobsterpots to block their path.

"Time to take me too," she said to the pair.

Phoenix and Polly looked at each other and nodded their heads. The three moved slowly along the harbour wall when Rory caught up with them.

"And me," he said.

Lady Arwen replied, "Come along."

As they made their way onto the beach, Kye appeared.

"I know where you are going," he said, "be careful."

Phoenix and Polly replied, "We will, see you later."

Lady Arwen simply said, "Bye Kye," and on they went.

After a long walk they came to a cave at the foot of the cliffs.

"This is where Kye showed us the entrance," said Phoenix. "We found him quivering and shivering and he told

32

us not to go in. But you probably know about cats and curiosity. Are you ready? Follow me."

Phoenix and Polly disappeared into the darkness followed by Lady Arwen and Rory.

Rory could see several barrels piled up in the cave.

"What's in those?" he said to Phoenix. "Brandy, lots of it," replied Phoenix, "belonging to the Pirates."

"You've been listening to too many bedtime stories!" laughed Rory.

At that moment, a bright light flooded the cave.

"Quick! Run!" hissed Phoenix to Rory and Lady Arwen, who darted behind a big rock.

"Ahoy Me Hearties!" bellowed a big man with a black beard, "I've been awaiting your return. Come on Lad and Lass, time to board the Ship."

Phoenix and Polly followed the Pirate as he carried one of the barrels out of the cave. Rory and Lady Arwen trailed behind and watched him load the barrel onto a rowing boat. Phoenix and Polly jumped on board and the Pirate returned for another barrel. Phoenix beckoned Rory and Lady Arwen to join them. As the Pirate returned, Polly hid the two under a tarpaulin. Three more pirates appeared and when all the barrels were loaded, they rowed the boat out to a very fine Pirate Ship.

The Pirates hoisted the barrels onto the deck whilst Phoenix and Polly scrabbled up the side of the Ship. Polly's extra digits proved very useful for the climb. While the Pirates were distracted, Rory gently pushed Lady Arwen into an open window low down on the Ship. He then followed his friends up onto the deck.

As he stood catching his breath, another large Pirate exclaimed, "Avast Ye! We appear to have a scurvy cat aboard!"

Remembering what Lady Arwen had told him, Rory decided to bravely approach the Pirate and bring the Ship good luck. The Pirate started to smile and all was well until another Pirate appeared carrying Lady Arwen.

This Pirate called out, "Cap'n, look at this Bilge Rat I've found below deck!"

Rory hated to see Lady Arwen being handled so roughly and he turned away from the Pirate Captain to help his friend. The smile disappeared from the captain's face and was replaced by a look of horror.

"Nooo! He walked away! That's real bad luck – to the Ship AND to you darned cat!"

Rory flew at the Pirate holding Lady Arwen, digging sharp claws into his leg. With a yowl, the Pirate dropped his captive and Rory rushed Lady Arwen to the side of the Ship.

"Let's go," he cried.

The two set off along a wooden plank just as Rory realised the Ship had set sail. There was nothing but water surrounding them.

Reaching the end of the plank, Rory saw a startled Phoenix and Polly watching from the deck.

The Ship was rocking wildly and, as the pair started to lose their footing, Rory called out, "Take care in the storm – you will return to Mulovelly."

Then SPLASH!

Rory found himself walking on the bottom of the sea alongside Lady Arwen. Being Purl Cats, they were able to do that.

"Wow, this is amazing!"

"True," replied Lady Arwen. "Look, there's a catfish"

"A catfish! He looks nothing like a cat!" exclaimed Rory as he peered at the strange looking fish.

"There's a dogfish," said Lady Arwen.

"You're kidding me!" laughed Rory. "He looks like a shark!"

"Oh, and there's an Angel Fish," whispered Lady Arwen.

Rory looked at the beautiful bright blue and yellow stripped fish as it swam slowly passed.

"There they are, Rory. The Purl Flaps"

Lady Arwen looked at Rory and said, "It's been an absolute pleasure knowing you, young man. I wish you much luck in your next adventures."

She moved to the Purrmanent Purl Flap and completed her journey.

Rory followed but found the Flap had locked behind her.

"Not my time yet," he muttered as he turned to the Tempurrary Flap and pushed through.

Chapter 5
SeaCat

As he emerged from the Purl Flap, Rory noticed he now sported a shiny, black coat with white splodges – and quite an impressive set of whiskers. The sun felt warm on his back. There were people hurrying in all directions around him, so he scampered under a wooden table set against a wall. From this shady refuge, he surveyed the scene before him.

Through the flying feet he could see a massive, grey metal ship with turrets and huge guns sticking up and out of it. At that moment, two things occurred, he realised he was very hungry and lunch flashed past him at considerable speed. He darted after the furry body and scaly tail.

With the meal and restorative ablutions complete, Rory needed a snooze. Now back under the wooden table, he was about to complete his third pre-curl up circle when a hand gently scooped him up and he found himself nose to nose with a young man in sailor's uniform.

"Hey Mate, I've been watching you – good job with that rat!"

The young sailor introduced himself as Ordinary Seaman George.

"Young cat, you are exactly what The Amethyst needs right now, you're hired!"

Although a little perplexed, Rory felt safe in George's arms and he began to relax.

As the two of them approached the big grey ship, George said, "I need to hide you, Mate, you're not currently on the guest list!"

Tucking his new friend inside his jacket, George marched up the gangway and made his way inside the Ship. Eventually, he sat down on a narrow bed in a rather cramped dark space.

"Well Mate, you're not going to miss Hong Kong at all. This is HMS Amethyst – we're a warship trying to keep some calm and help our friends stay out of trouble in these dodgy times."

In the gloom, Rory could make out two long rows of beds separated by raggedy curtains.

"These are our bunks," chipped in George. "There's nearly 200 of us on board and it can get a bit hot and smelly but I'm sure you'll fit in really well! And the Captain's cabin is just over there – he's going to love you."

George went on to explain that mealtimes were the highlight of their day, but a problem with onboard rodents was causing increasing issues with the rations.

"Seeing your skills in action, Mate, you are now appointed Ship's Ratter – what d'ya think?"

Rory was contemplating the implications of the honour bestowed when George followed up with, "and you need a name! I'm going to call you Simon – that seems to suit you!"

So, Rory became Simon and his new life in Rodent Control settled down nicely. The sailors took it in turns to bring snacks from their rations to help vary his diet. Early on, he was introduced to the captain whose stern gaze immediately adopted a slightly far away glaze. Realising that Captain Griffiths had a soft spot for him, Simon upgraded his accommodation to the Captain's Cabin although he still saw George every day. The on-board rats were rather fat and easy to capture. Simon frequently presented a choice selection to the captain in person, although the one he deposited on his bunk was not quite as well received. When not on Ratting Duties, Simon's favourite place to snooze was in the Captain's Cabin, curled up inside the captain's cap.

Captain Griffiths and Simon often undertook regular Ship's Inspection together. The captain only had to whistle for his feline friend and he was there, Simon checking for possible rat routes and the captain, well, for everything else.

Simon overheard conversations about conflict and ceasefire but, generally, life continued at the same pace for many months. Captain Griffiths left the Ship and was replaced by Captain Skinner who thankfully also liked cats. Although the new Captain did whistle for Simon's company at

Inspection Time, it just wasn't the same and he politely declined.

Then, one day, the Ship started to move.

Captain Skinner appeared in the cabin to gently remove his cap from under Simon, explaining, "We're on our way from Shanghai to Nanking to relieve HMS Consort. No trouble expected, so carry on snoozing Simon."

A few hours later, Simon was contemplating his next Ratting shift when he found himself flying across the cabin amidst screeching pieces of metal, orange flames and black smoke. The noise of the explosion hurt his ears and the smell and heat were terrifying. A heavy landing whisked his breath away.

As the bombardment continued overhead, Simon felt himself slipping away to a more peaceful place. He caught sight of the Purl Flaps drifting in and out of his peripheral vision and he prepared for exit. Feeling more like Rory, he hovered in-between for some time, but something was pulling him back to Simon. Eventually, Simon opened his eyes.

Although everything hurt, he realised he was very thirsty and, following a chink of light, made his way onto a vastly different Ship's deck.

He couldn't hear Petty Officer Murray exclaim, "Simon! Good grief – where have you been for the last two days?"

A large, soot-covered hand carefully lifted the injured cat and cradled him until they reached the Sick Bay. The Medical Officer assessed the wounds to his body and burns to his face whilst Simon gratefully lapped some water. His fine set of whiskers had also suffered with one side missing and the other all curled up and singed.

All the injured sailors had already been treated or evacuated, so surgery followed swiftly. When he awoke, he overheard the Medical Officer explaining to George that there had been several pieces of metal removed and his burns treated. The medic also thought that Simon's heart had been weakened and he wasn't sure he would make it through the next day. Simon, however, had other ideas and set his sights on returning to duty.

He remained in the Sick Bay whilst his wounds started to heal. Simon saw the haunted looks on the faces of the injured sailors – all traumatised by the unexpected attack on The Amethyst and the loss of their colleagues. When he was well enough, Simon would nestle in the crook of a sailor's elbow, hold the young man's gaze, undertake some important kneading and purr gently. Because he had also been injured, Simon was considered one of them.

He never saw Captain Skinner again and, unfortunately, his replacement, Captain Kerans, was not a cat lover. When Simon attempted to return to his old haunts and routines, the new boss hastily ejected him from both his cabin and his cap.

As his strength grew, Simon returned to Ratting Duties. In his absence, the rodents had started to invade the living quarters, breed ferociously and consume voraciously.

Over the next three months, The Amethyst was prevented from sailing due to the ongoing conflict. By this stage, the Ship's rations were becoming scarce and precious. Simon met his target of at least one rat a day and often more which also contributed to raising on-board morale.

Deciding it was time to win over Captain Kerans, Simon presented him with his daily catch. Uncertain quite what to do, the captain stroked him, and then threw the rat overboard when Simon wasn't watching. A while later, when the captain caught a virus and was confined to bed, Simon saw his chance and jumped up on his bunk. This time he was permitted to stay and indeed sleep wherever he wished from then on.

There was a particularly large and vicious rat causing havoc with the supplies.

The crew named him, 'Mao Tse-tung.'

He had evaded all attempts to trap him and it was felt that Simon would not be able to cope with the task. However, one day the two came face-to-face: Simon sprang first and killed the rat outright. The delighted crew hailed him as a hero, and he was promoted to Able SeaCat Simon.

The lockdown continued for several weeks. With available rations and morale very low and the heat and humidity very high, Simon did his best to help. His ratting skills and his ability to bring a smile were hugely appreciated.

Eventually, when The Amethyst was dangerously low on fuel, Captain Kerans saw only one possible solution – make a run for it. So, on a hot, moonless night, the Ship's engines started up and they headed for open sea.

A few hours later, the captain was able to announce, 'We have re-joined the fleet – no damage or casualties – God save the King.'

Simon felt the relief of the crew as they cuddled and petted him amongst smiles and tears.

A presentation was made on the deck recognising the achievements of all on-board. Whilst the crew stood to attention, the Ship's Ratter was gently held by a young seaman and Able SeaCat Simon was awarded the Amethyst Campaign Ribbon.

As the Ship was repaired, news of the whole event spread back to the UK and it was decided that Simon should be awarded the Dickin Medal – the PDSA animal award for gallantry. A special collar in the colours of the medal ribbon was sent for Simon to wear and he was due to be presented with a temporary, home-made medal – but he didn't fancy that and bolted.

When they eventually arrived back home, Simon became a celebrity receiving over 200 messages in the post every day. He wasn't too keen on the photographers with their flashing cameras and often shot out of sight. Nevertheless, many pictures did appear, including in Time magazine, of the once again handsome cat with an almost full set of whiskers.

Simon was very spoilt during his six months of compulsory quarantine. He relished the attention but towards the end of the period, found himself feeling listless and not quite himself.

A date was set for Simon to be presented by the Lord Mayor of London with the proper Dickin medal and preparations were well under way. His adoring, 'cat officer,' began to realise that all was not well and that Simon's little heart, having undergone such a traumatic experience, was struggling. The worried officer decided to read out to Simon part of the medal testimonial letter from the Captain of the Amethyst:

'Throughout the incident, Simon's behaviour was of the highest order. One would not have expected a small cat to survive the blast from an explosion capable of making a hole over a foot in diameter in a steel plate. Yet, after a few days, Simon was as friendly as ever. His presence on the Ship was a deciding factor in maintaining the high level of morale of the Ship's company.'

Simon, safe and loved, drifted off into sleep.

This time, the Purl flaps appeared solid and fully in focus. Gathering strength from anticipation and the return of Rory, he ignored the Purrmanent Flap and pushed through the familiar gateway.

Chapter 6
Memories

It took some effort for Rory to push through the Purl flap.

"That's strange," he thought to himself, "it's never been this hard before."

He glanced down at his coat to assess the form of this reincarnation.

"Well, there we go," he exclaimed, "I thought it might happen at some stage!"

The tortoiseshell fur said it all, "I'm a female!"

Her body felt tired and well-used, her once colourful coat was tatty and dusty and the vision from one eye was a little sqiffy.

"This could be interesting!"

She made her way slowly around the perimeter of a yard filled with junk metal and rubber tyres, wincing as one of her hips was giving her gip. There were rusty cars piled on top of each other, several truck skeletons and the remains of an old bus.

Hearing a commotion from the middle of the yard, she backed into the shadows and through rheumy eyes observed a large group of cats chasing each other and performing catrobatic leaps and tight turns. They were predominantly, but not exclusively, Exhuberants – that age between kitten and adult where there's too much energy and too little experience.

Transfixed by the catrobatics, she didn't see three Exhuberants approaching out of the gloom. A terrifying guttural hiss took her by surprise followed by the loudest, sonorous yowl which was shared by the trio.

"What is it, Posh?" ventured one. "It smells as bad as it looks!"
After allowing a few seconds to assess the situation, the pure white Exhuberant's eyes opened wide.

She took a sharp intake of breath, "Oh my goodness, Darcee, she's back! She's had the catawall to come back!"

"Who's come back from where?" ventured TiramuSue.

"Catabella!" spat Posh. "Don't touch her – she has a most dubious past and we are not allowed to go near her – she can't be trusted!"

Struggling to access even the slightest memory of her days gone by, Catabella decided it would be prudent to withdraw from the uncomfortable situation and reverse into the shadows. The Exhuberants were so occupied with their own expressions and responses that by the time they looked for the old cat, she had disappeared.

From the relative safety of a worn-out tyre, Catabella watched as a rather matronly cat approached.

The Exhuberants were still far too busy whispering behind their paws to notice until, "Where have you three been? Have you forgotten what an important night this is? Old Moses is getting ready to make his choice and all the Catdidates are nervous and need entertaining!"

Posh jumped before replying, "Oh sorry, Leigh – we'll be right back. Did you see that Catabella has returned?"

"What!" exclaimed the older cat. "Are you sure? After all this time – why would she come back…. unless….?"

Leigh scratched her ear in contemplation, "I need to talk to Old Moses – Posh and Darcee, are you ready, TiramuSue, please keep a lookout for Catabella – we don't want any unexpected reunions or confrontations especially tonight."

As the cats scattered, Catabella popped her head above the rim of the tyre and found that she had a pretty good view of the junk yard below. A fizzle of a memory stirred within her.

"Old Moses, eh? He wasn't so old the last time I saw him. I seem to recall that he was quite a kitten-daddy – and a good one at that, certainly for my own my own litterings."

Her gaze misted over as she struggled to fill the large gaps floating just outside her recollection. Shivering under her thinning coat in the night chill, she thought of many days spent curled up in the warmth of the sun.

"I was beautiful then," she mused.

Catabella watched as a cat hidden from view announced the performances of Posh and Darcee who jumped and danced across the arena with energy and grace.

The elderly cat felt flickers of recollection dart from ears to tail. She struggled to make sense of it all – until the cat announcer stepped out of the shadows.

"Oh, my goodness!" she gulped, "it's Moriarty!"

Catabella hadn't noticed that TiramaSue had crept back and was quietly sitting beside her.

"Are you alright?" the Exhuberant ventured.

"No, not really," replied a clearly shaken Catabella. "I've been struggling with some massive holes in my memory – then I saw Moriarty – and it all came yowling back! Look, it's made my fur stand on end!"

"He's certainly a bad boy," replied TiramaSue. "I've managed to stay out of his grasp – so far – but, he's not one you can say 'No' to, for long."

"I know, he and I have history – I wasn't strong enough to reject him."

Catabella stared at her raggedy paws and then at TiramaSue's who was sitting four-paw-neat. Watching the old cat's gaze, the Exhuberant folded her front paws inwards and sank down to a more comfortable position. Catabella followed suit.

With the evening entertainment continuing below, TiramaSue focused on her distressed companion, "Tell me about it."

"The memories have come flooding back although I'm really struggling with what's happening at the moment. I can't even remember how I got here or what I'm supposed to be doing."

TiramaSue said nothing, tilting her head to encourage Catabella.

"It all started with the catnip," she continued, "and, wow, it was good stuff! Very soon you found that, after a chomp, everything was much more colourful, more fun – you felt totally alive! You'd lose all your inhibitions. That's when I went from being a beautiful Exhuberant to a shunned creature of the night. When I asked if I could go back, Moriarty just laughed and left a deep scratch on my nose."

"Oh, that's so sad – I promise you I will never take catnip or go near that criminal of a cat."

A little smile appeared on Catabella's face although TiramaSue wasn't sure whether the wetness on her cheek was tears or just her leaky eyes.

"Tell me what else you remember – from before that terrible time."

The old cat settled herself and wrapped her tail around her frail form.

"I remember the instructions given to us as new Exhuberants. How a cat should expect respect from its humans – and before we became a trusted friend, we should receive many tokens of esteem – like bowls of milk – or even cream."

On a bit of a roll now, she continued, "And, of course, there's our names – three in total. First is the name our human family give us – mine was Velcro – apparently due to my sharp claws catching on everything. Secondly, our particular feline name – as you know, mine's Catabella. And finally, our secret ineffable name known only to ourselves."

For reasons she couldn't identify, the name Rory popped into her mind – but she left it there for later.

"See, you do have some great memories and I'm sure you were a very glamorous cat before the hard times."

"Thank you for your kind words," replied the old cat. "It's a shame I made some bad decisions which caused me to be rejected and expelled from the colony."

"Are you aware of the importance of tonight?"

"Yes," replied Catabella, "it's coming back to me – one night every year the Senior Respect selects a deserving cat to fast-track to the Purl Flap and be reborn into a new, better life."

"That's right – and there are several eager Catdidates vying for the honour. Moriarty is convinced he can be regenerated into an even more evil version of himself!"

Suddenly, there was a flurry of activity in the arena. Leigh came rushing up – she was breathless and in a panic.

"Old Moses has been catnapped! I'd just told him you'd come back and he turned away from me saying he had something in his eye. Moriarty overheard and guided Moses into the shadows saying he was going to sort his eye out – and now the two of them have disappeared!"

"Looks like we need Dynamo!" exclaimed TiramaSue.

"Who's Dynamo?" asked Catabella.

"Dynamo is the absolute opposite of Moriarty – he's a good boy, a great problem solver and a bit of a magician – if a little gullible at times. He even has the ability to disappear into thin air. In fact, not long ago, he said he'd found a hidden supply of very tasty food – pilchards, I think it was – and then he just disappeared completely for a day or so before reappearing just as instantly. Mind you, he didn't seem quite the same on his return."

"If anyone can find Old Moses, Dynamo can and will!"

Posh stepped out from behind a rusty oilcan, "I've been listening to you talking with TiramaSue and I want to say I'm so sorry for what I said and for judging you so harshly. Will you come down with me into the arena and share some more of your stories with the rest of the Exhuberants and Catdidates."

The atmosphere changed completely as Catabella recounted her memories – it wasn't just the old cat's eyes which leaked profusely – and paws reached out to touch and stroke the thinning, tortoiseshell fur. A peaceful harmony enveloped the arena until the spell was broken by a loud crash as a handsome black cat appeared gently leading the missing Senior Respect, Old Moses.

"Dynamo! Dynamo!" the chant went up from the masses, "Magical Dynamo!"

Old Moses raised a large paw and silence occurred.

"Apologies for the delay on this special night," he said. "I realise there are several Catdidates hoping to persuade me this is their time – some more deserving than others, I must say. I have now made my choice."

Old Moses stepped slowly forwards, took Catabella by the paw and accompanied her to the base of the now glowing ramp leading to the Purl Flaps.

As she started her slow ascent, she looked around for any sign of Moriarty – but he was gone.

The rest of the cats stood quietly watching the old cat complete her journey. As Catabella started to fade, Rory began his return.

He reached the Purl Flap and mused to himself, "One day, they'll probably make something of this story – maybe even set it to music."

Then he pushed through.

Chapter 7
Stray Cats

This time, the push through was easy. Rory was contemplating how these re-entries were both familiar and totally unfamiliar, when a squirrel shot past giving a stern look whilst muttering, "Not another one!"

Stepping out of the bushes onto an extensive area of grass, he saw people, some walking purposefully, some strolling in the warm sunshine, some sitting on the grass, laughing, eating and drinking. A stretch of water nestled amid the green and the area was surrounded by tall buildings and noisy traffic.

Rory watched as the squirrel moved from one seated group to another, accepting morsels of food with over-exaggerated grace.

Eventually, the sun began to set over the trees and buildings. Rory withdrew into the bushes where he spent a chilly night. Emerging the next morning, he finally acknowledged his new livery – predominantly white with a ginger cap and rear end – 'sort of Whinger,' he mused.

Exploring the locality, he found a brick path, fenced off to the public. It crossed over the duck-filled water to a small island offering night-time shelter. Over the next couple of days, he discovered he could dine well, small furies as starters, larger, feathered entrees and picnic remains for dessert. Life would be good this time around.

Occasionally, he saw the squirrel but he kept his distance.

A few days later, he spotted a tabby and white cat strolling across the lawns. Unsure of the potential outcome, he hesitated. The cat continued his approach looking completely laid back.

"Good morning."

"Hi," replied Rory.

"Do you reside here, my good fellow?"

"Er, yes," replied Rory. "Why are you talking like that?"

"Oh sorry, I seem to have picked it up from my owner. She lives across the road there in one of those big white houses."

Rory glanced in the direction the cat was gesturing, "Goodness, that looks impressive – why do you come over here?"

"Oh man, I really need my own space and freedom," he replied in a much more normal tone. "She's a lovely lady – but it's just not what I'm used to, particularly after my last regeneration."

"You're a Purl Cat too," said Rory, "very pleased to make your acquaintance – what do I call you?"

"My lady calls me Tarquin, but that's so not me. I didn't have a name in my real life as I lived on the streets a very long time ago. The first one I recall is Hodge, will that do?"

"Absolutely – I'm Rory."

The two became firm friends, firstly in the park and later, venturing beyond its boundaries to explore the city of London.

Hodge took Rory to a statue of a cat sitting next to a pair of empty oyster shells.

"That's to commemorate me," he said simply. "I was owned by a famous writer called Samuel Johnson – he used to go out and buy me oysters to eat, very tasty, I must say! He wrote some poems about me and even today, people leave coins in the oyster shells and occasionally tie ribbons around my neck."

Rory was impressed and told Hodge about his time as Able SeaCat Simon and the surreal experience of being Catabella.

Hodge responded with the strangest of all Purl Cat experiences. He related the time he became Kasper, the Savoy Hotel Cat. Apparently, there had been a special meal at the hotel where one guest didn't turn up leaving 13 diners. It was noted at the time that this was an unlucky number and shortly afterwards one of the 13 was shot dead.

To avoid adverse publicity which could damage their reputation, the Savoy had a statue made of a black cat which was brought out every time there was a party of thirteen. Kasper would have a napkin tied around his neck and be served every course, just like the other guests.

Winston Churchill had been very fond of him and, when, during World War 2, he was catnapped by some mischievous Royal Air Force personnel and flown to Singapore, Churchill demanded that he be returned immediately.

Hodge said he had spent a very surreal but fascinating time observing the habits of the rich and famous.

Over the following months, the two spent a lot of time together. Hodge would return to his owner and become Tarquin for a while but, before long, his need for freedom and his internal catnav brought him back to the park and Rory.

On one of their meanders around the city, Hodge took Rory to a quiet street with big black gates at one end.

"I want to introduce you to another friend. He's called Larry and he looks a lot like me – in fact, I'm often mistaken for his doppelcatter."

"Well hello, my little Spiegel."

Hodge nearly jumped out of his skin as an equally tabby and white cat appeared from nowhere.

"Now, are we being Tarquin today?" said the cat in a very Tarquin voice, "or me old mucker, Hodge?" he finished in a more colloquial tone.

"For goodness's sake, Larry, don't do that, you nearly received the reactionary claw!" Hodge let his fur settle down for a moment before introducing Rory as his Purl Cat friend.

"Ah, fascinating, I've only met a few, as far as I'm aware, but of course, Purl Cats don't always share this news. I'm Larry, Chief Mouser to the Cabinet Office and I assume that you are the reason I've not seen much of my speigeltwin recently?"

Rory tried to look apologetic but didn't really feel he pulled it off.

"I need Hodge so that I can remain on top of the rodent issue – every great leader has his team enabling him to be effective."

"You mean, I work hard to achieve your quota, and you get all the glory," exclaimed Hodge.

Rory started to think there was going to be fistypaws when he saw a wink pass between the virtually identical moggies.

"You always get on better with Palmerston," said Larry, "he constantly riles me claiming he has a grander title – Chief Mouser to the Foreign and Commonwealth Office – for goodness's sake, he's hopeless!"

"I wouldn't concern yourself with Palmerston, Larry, he's not the brightest feline. I still think he can't tell us apart – he's crossed claws with both of us and, anyway, he's about to be retired off," laughed Hodge.

"He is handy, though, for recalling the tales of your predecessors. Let me see, before you there was Sybil – that didn't last too long – she hated London and was sent to live in Scotland. And before her, was Humphrey."

"Yes, he lasted three Prime Ministers and was photographed on the steps of Number 10 more often than I am!" exclaimed Larry.

"They also thought he had killed some Robin chicks – which he hadn't – and savaging a duck in the park – which he had," continued Hodge.

"Ooops," whispered Rory, as he had dined on park duck a few times.

"Humphrey finally retired in 1997 after an alleged rift with Cherie Blair – and, after Sybil's brief tenure, I was selected from Battersea to become Chief Mouser at Number 10."

With the storytelling complete, Hodge and Rory left Downing Street although they returned on a regular basis – Hodge more often than Rory – and life settled down into a balance of work, rest and play.

After a chilly and rather wet winter, spring arrived and something odd happened. Virtually overnight, all the people and traffic disappeared. The lack of background noise was a welcome benefit but the lack of picnickers was a serious handicap to a varied diet. The prolonged glares from the squirrel clearly indicated he blamed Rory for the dearth of his regular morsels. However, the local wildlife became bolder and accessible although Rory did leave the ducks alone.

Larry was safe and well-fed but he did mention to Hodge and Rory that he'd been severely alarmed on several occasions when, "the flop-haired man," had insisted on clapping loudly just as he had been on Mousing Duties.

Eventually, the strollers and picnickers began to return, although in far fewer numbers, and the reduced traffic noise took on a new normality.

Hodge and Rory spent many months exploring together. One afternoon in the park, Hodge turned to his friend, "My owner's been feeling lonely during this weird time so I need to be more Tarquin for a while. And you, my Purl Cat friend, are starting to look a little tired. Maybe it's time to move on?"

Rory took a deep breath and gave a little nod.

Sitting side by side, they watched as a man with long grey hair took a guitar from its case and, perching on the grass, began to strum and sing.

Rory leaned over to Hodge and asked, "Do you think the words of these songs change as the singer get older? How about, 'Hey You, Get Off My Commode', or 'Hi, Ho, Panty Lining', or 'Born to Be Riled', or 'Portaloo Sunset'?"

Not receiving a response, he glanced at Hodge and saw a far-away look in his eyes, "Wow, this brings back so many memories."

"Are you okay, fella?"

"I didn't tell you about my previous regeneration, did I?"

"No – you just mentioned that you were used to having your freedom."

"I was feral, quite a handsome ginger. Then I hurt my leg, it was so painful. Wandering around for somewhere safe to hide, I saw this scruffy man who sat with me talking softly. He looked in a worse state than I was but he picked me up and looked after me. He also had a guitar in a case and when my leg recovered, I'd follow and sit with him when he played. We even travelled on the bus together and I loved perching on his shoulder. I heard him say that I saved his life, but, quite honestly, it was the other way around. His name was James and he called me Bob."

Leaving his friend lost in memories, Rory retreated into the park bushes.

Turning, first he saw the squirrel who gave a tail twitch and said, "Just making sure you are going!"

Then he gave a sigh and pushed through the familiar Purl Flap.

Chapter 8
No Regrets

The push through was more snug than usual. Rory glanced back at the Purl Flap which had not altered in size, "perhaps, I've developed some muscles, at last!" he muttered.

Before he could assess his new presentation, he found himself gently floating across a space packed with machinery, cables and wires.

"Whoa, this is really weird – fun, but weird!"

He gently bounced off the side wall, rose to the ceiling and sank down to the floor.

Through an archway, he heard a sound and, making slow progress, moved towards it.

Peering into another area filled with dials, knobs and gauges, he saw a man easing out of some bulky white clothing whilst complaining, "This flippin' Spacesuit was definitely made for a female!"

Hearing Rory's approach, the man turned and smiled, "Well I never, a Lynx – how appropriate is that!"

Rory caught sight of himself in the shiny front of a metal box.

A large, sturdy cat with sandy-grey markings and black tufted ears looked back at him, "Oh, how handsome am I," he gasped, "though, not much of a tail to speak of!"

"Lynx, let me introduce myself," said the man as he floated towards Rory. "I'm Tim – not Tim Peake – but another Tim from many years earlier. I used to fly Lynx helicopters in the Army Air Corp. One day I heard something amazing on the radio 'Astronaut wanted – no experience required.' I applied, along with thousands of other hopefuls, and eventually two of us were selected to go to Russia and prepare for The Juno Mission."

Tim explained he learned to speak Russian and underwent the tough cosmonaut training. He said he and the other finalist knew that only one of them would end up going into space – and they had both stated they would be happy for the other to be chosen.

Three days before 'lift off' the decision was made and, on the 18th May 1991, Helen Sharman blasted off to the Russian Space Station, Mir.

Tim said he managed to contain his emotions at the time although, when asked a few weeks later whether he was disappointed, he had replied, "Only terminally!"

After executing a perfect somersault, Tim added, "But life went on and most of it was wonderful – I married the daughter of a Russian Cosmonaut and flew Nelson Mandela around by helicopter in South Africa."

Floating slowly upwards, he continued, "Of course, life is rarely perfect, and there's no doubt in my mind that, when we approach the end of our time as a tourist on earth – or even above the earth – we need to sort out any regrets, and either park them or punch them into action."

Tim excused himself telling Lynx that he had several experiments to complete in the next chamber of the Space Station. Left alone, Lynx attempted a somersault of his own but discovered that four gangly legs did not make the process achievable or elegant. When he had regained some dignity, he reflected on his own time as an earth tourist.

"I don't have any regrets. During my real life and my eight regenerations, I have tried to be helpful and, most importantly, I've been a good and loyal friend. What else is there of any significance?"

After a short while, Tim bobbed back explaining his work was done. He had a look of calm contentment as he explained how, a few months earlier, he had become ill and it was clear recovery was not an option.

"I'd heard, when people begin to approach the completion of their journey, they often experience vivid dreams which enable them to punch a parked regret into action. I want to thank you, Lynx, for sharing this amazing dream with me."

Tim turned and made his way into the last of the chambers. Lynx floated after but immediately realised that Tim had made his exit and was gone.

As the muscles receded and the tail extended, Rory began his last return. He saw the two Purl Flaps. This time, the

Tempurrary Flap was firmly shut whilst the Purrmanent Flap sat ajar.

With a long, exhaled breath and a sense of closure, he pushed through.